Disney

Pooh's Hone

Written by
Guy Davis

Illustrated by
Costa Alavezos

Published by
Louis Weber, C.E.O., Publications International, Ltd.
7373 North Cicero Avenue, Lincolnwood, Illinois 60712

Ground Floor, 59 Gloucester Place, London W1U 8JJ

Customer Service: 1-800-595-8484 or customer_service@pilbooks.com

www.pilbooks.com

p i kids is a registered trademark of Publications International, Ltd.

Manufactured in China.
ISBN-13: 978-1-4127-3021-1
ISBN-10: 1-4127-3021-X

Winnie the Pooh was hungry. And when Pooh felt rumbly in his tumbly, honey was what he was hungry for.

So Pooh began to search high and low for some honey. But all of his honey pots were empty! Where could he find some honey?

"Hello, Rabbit, old friend," Pooh called out to his neighbor.

"Hello, Pooh," replied Rabbit.

"Rabbit, do you think that you might have a smackerel of honey?" asked Pooh.

KeRiTs

Before Rabbit could answer, Pooh asked another question.

"Why are you always working in the garden, Rabbit? Wouldn't you enjoy a nice lunch instead?"

"The garden *is* my lunch!" replied Rabbit cheerfully.

KeRiTs

Rabbit decided to give Pooh a tour of his garden.

"You see, Pooh, there are lots of delicious fruits and vegetables growing here," explained Rabbit. "Some come from seeds, and grow into plants that bear fruit. Other seeds grow up to become trees."

"And some plants," Rabbit continued, "like carrots and potatoes, grow under the ground."

Then Rabbit showed Pooh how to care for the soil, how to plant a seed, and how to water a plant.

"That's it!" thought Pooh. "I'll plant a honeypot, and then I can grow all the honey I could ever want!"

The very idea of a huge honey tree dripping with delicious golden honey made Pooh grin from ear to ear. Pooh was eager to share his great plan with Rabbit.

"Pooh, that's preposterous!" blurted Rabbit.

"You're right," replied Pooh. "First I must plant a little honeypot." So Pooh borrowed a honeypot from Rabbit, dug a hole, and planted it.

Rabbit sighed. "This won't work."

"Quite right," Pooh agreed. "Without water, it will never grow! Thank you, Rabbit!"

HUNNY
TREE

Pooh checked on his honey tree every day. Soon Pooh began to wonder why his honey tree wasn't growing.

One afternoon, a big rainstorm blew in. "Maybe this is exactly what my honey tree needs to grow," Pooh thought as he hurried home.

HUNNY
TREE

Pooh sat patiently and looked out his window during the storm. When it ended, Pooh rushed back to check on his honey tree.

But the blustery rainstorm had blown away his honey tree marker! Pooh looked everywhere, but he could not find the spot where he had planted Rabbit's little honeypot.

HUNNY
TREE

Just then, Pooh spotted a tree he had never seen before. It was a great big tree, and from it hung two great big beehives.

"There you are," grinned Pooh. "There's my honey tree!"

Later, Pooh loved to tell his friends the story of his honey tree, and how he grew it from a tiny little honeypot.

And whenever Pooh told the tale, Rabbit would just shake his head.